Margaret L. Woods

Lyrics and Ballads

Margaret L. Woods

Lyrics and Ballads

ISBN/EAN: 9783744787574

Printed in Europe, USA, Canada, Australia, Japan

Cover: Foto ©Andreas Hilbeck / pixelio.de

More available books at **www.hansebooks.com**

LYRICS AND BALLADS

LYRICS & BALLADS

BY

MARGARET L. WOODS

AUTHOR OF 'A VILLAGE TRAGEDY'

LONDON

RICHARD BENTLEY & SON

𝔓𝔲𝔟𝔩𝔦𝔰𝔥𝔢𝔯𝔰 𝔦𝔫 𝔒𝔯𝔡𝔦𝔫𝔞𝔯𝔶 𝔱𝔬 𝔥𝔢𝔯 𝔐𝔞𝔧𝔢𝔰𝔱𝔶 𝔱𝔥𝔢 ℭ𝔲𝔢𝔢𝔫

1889

TO

My Father and Mother

CONTENTS

CONTENTS

REST

To spend the long warm days
Silent beside the silent-stealing streams,
To see, not gaze,
To hear, not listen, thoughts exchanged for dreams :

See clouds that slowly pass
Trailing their shadows o'er the far faint down,
And ripening grass,
While yet the meadows wear their starry crown :

To hear the breezes sigh
Cool in the silver leaves like falling rain,
Pause and go by,
Tired wanderers o'er the solitary plain :

See far from all affright

Shy river creatures play hour after hour,

And night by night

Low in the West the white moon's folding flower.

Thus lost to human things,

To blend at last with Nature and to hear

What song she sings

Low to herself when there is no one near.

TO THE FORGOTTEN DEAD

To the forgotten dead,

Come, let us drink in silence ere we part.

To every fervent yet resolvèd heart

That brought its tameless passion and its tears,

Renunciation and laborious years,

To lay the deep foundations of our race,

To rear its stately fabric overhead

And light its pinnacles with golden grace.

To the unhonoured dead.

To the forgotten dead,

Whose dauntless hands were stretched to grasp the rein

Of Fate and hurl into the void again

Her thunder-hoofèd horses, rushing blind

Earthward along the courses of the wind.

Among the stars, along the wind in vain

Their souls were scattered and their blood was shed,

And nothing, nothing of them doth remain.

> To the thrice-perished dead.

L'ENVOI

LIKE the wreath the poet sent
 To the lady of old time,
Roses that were discontent
 With their brief unhonoured prime,
 Crown he hoped she might endow
 With the beauty of her brow;
Even so for you I blent,
Send to you my wreath of rhyme.

These alas ! be blooms less bright,
 Faded buds that never blew,
Darkling thoughts that seek the light—
 Let them find it finding you.

Bid these petals pale unfold

On your heart their hearts of gold,

Sweetness for your sole delight,

Love for odour, tears for dew.

GAUDEAMUS IGITUR

Come, no more of grief and dying!

Sing the time too swiftly flying.

> Just an hour
>
> Youth's in flower,

Give me roses to remember

In the shadow of December.

Fie on steeds with leaden paces!

Winds shall bear us on our races,

> Speed, O speed,
>
> Wind, my steed,

Beat the lightning for your master,

Yet my Fancy shall fly faster.

Give me music, give me rapture,

Youth that's fled can none recapture;

   Not with thought

   Wisdom's bought.

Out on pride and scorn and sadness!

Give me laughter, give me gladness.

Sweetest Earth, I love and love thee,

Seas about thee, skies above thee,

   Sun and storms,

   Hues and forms

Of the clouds with floating shadows

On thy mountains and thy meadows.

Earth, there's none that can enslave thee,

Not thy lords it is that have thee;

   Not for gold

   Art thou sold,

But thy lovers at their pleasure

Take thy beauty and thy treasure.

While sweet fancies meet me singing,

While the April blood is springing

      In my breast,

      While a jest

And my youth thou yet must leave me,

Fortune, 'tis not thou canst grieve me.

When at length the grasses cover

Me, the world's unwearied lover,

      If regret

      Haunt me yet,

It shall be for joys untasted,

Nature lent and folly wasted.

Youth and jests and summer weather,

Goods that kings and clowns together

Waste or use

As they choose,

These, the best, we miss pursuing

Sullen shades that mock our wooing.

Feigning Age will not delay it—

When the reckoning comes we'll pay it,

Own our mirth

Has been worth

All the forfeit light or heavy

Wintry Time and Fortune levy.

Feigning grief will not escape it,

What though ne'er so well you ape it—

Age and care

All must share,

All alike must pay hereafter,

Some for sighs and some for laughter.

Know, ye sons of Melancholy,

To be young and wise is folly.

'Tis the weak

Fear to wreak

On this clay of life their fancies,

Shaping battles, shaping dances.

While ye scorn our names unspoken,

Roses dead and garlands broken,

O ye wise,

We arise,

Out of failures, dreams, disasters,

We arise to be your masters.

THE SOWERS

Woe to the seed
    The winds carry
O'er fallow and mead !
    They do not tarry,

They seek the sea,
    The barren strand,
Where foam-flakes flee
    O'er the salt land.

Where the sharp spray
    And sand are blown,
In the wind's play
    The seed is sown.

Falling on shore

It cries, "The earth

Opens her door!

There shall be birth

"From thee far place,

From thee fair hour,

Splendour and grace

Of leaf and flower."

Falling on sea

It cries, "Again

Com'st thou to me,

Refreshing rain—

"Only more great,

More strong thou art

Like to my fate,

Like to my heart."

On barren shore,

Or sullen wave,

When storms are o'er

It finds a grave.

THE SONG OF THE LUTE PLAYER

STILL as a star came to my breast
    A joy unbidden,
  Not to be known, not to be guessed,
    So fair, so hidden ;
And now within 'tis like the starry night,
The unimagined pure ethereal height,
Trembling in loneliness at its own light.

  Heaven of my joy, fair though thou art,
    A light for ever,
  Yet there's a grief hid in my heart
    Like the great river.
At times a little while it seems to sleep,

C

And then a voice cries to it from the deep,

And all its floods over my spirit sweep.

Hast thou a joy?   Though but a flower

O maiden, bring it.

Though but a dream of morning hour,

Yet will I sing it.

And as a bird that calls its mate my strain

—Listen, the lute begins like falling rain—

Shall call the Spring and Spring return again.

Hast thou a fear hid in thy heart,

A sorrow sleeping?

Light though it be, soon to depart,

I'll sing it weeping.

The ruined shrines shall answer as I sing,

In hollow tombs of many an ancient king

Forgotten woes shall waken murmuring.

Then in my song, maiden, I'll weave

The world's emotion,

Passion of souls that laugh and grieve,

And Earth and Ocean.

The silver spheres shall hush awhile their quire,

Saying, " Return, lost star of our desire,

Lend us again thy music and thy fire."

Only my joy, only my pain

May not be spoken.

These would I tell, earthward again

The song drops broken.

Sleeping I dream my joy, my sorrow sing.

I wake—the lonely night is listening

To one long sigh, breathed·from a shattered string.

"AGAIN I SAW ANOTHER ANGEL"

I DREAMED a dream within a dream.

An angel cinctured with the gleam

Of topaz and of chrysoprase,

And circled with the lambent rays

That lightened from his sheathless sword,

Leapt into heaven's deserted ways,

And cried, "The message of the Lord."

Then suddenly the earth was white

With faces turned towards his light.

The nations' pale expectancy

Sobbed far beneath him like the sea,

But men exulted in their dread,

And drunken with an awful glee

Beat at the portals of the dead.

I saw this monstrous grave the earth

Shake with a spasm as though of birth,

And shudder with a sullen sound,

As though the dead stirred in the ground.

And that great angel girt with flame

Cried till the heavens were rent around,

" Come forth ye dead ! "—Yet no man came.

Then there was silence overhead :

But far below the ancient dead

Muttered as if in mockery ;

And there was darkness in the sky,

And rolling through the realm of death,

Laughter and some obscure reply,

With tongues that none interpreteth.

Ay, laugh ye undeluded dead !

The wrathful vintagers that tread

The wine-press of the world ye know.

How often shall your graves below

Rock to the thunder of their feet ?

The angels of the whirlwind sow

Fierce seed the children take for wheat ?

O seed of blood !   O seed of tears,

Thick sown through all our human years,

What harvest do the days return ?

New thorns to break, new tares to burn,

New angels sent on earth to reap.

This is the recompense we earn—

Lie still, ye dead, lie still and sleep.

A BALLADE OF THE NIGHT

FAR from the earth the deep-descended day

Lies dim in hidden sanctuaries of sleep.

The winged winds couched on the threshold keep

Uneasy watch, and still expectant stay

The voice that bids their rushing host delay

No more to rise, and with tempestuous power

Rend the wide veil of heaven.   Long watching they

Sigh in the silence of the midnight hour.

Hark ! where the forests slow in slumber sway

Below the blue wild ridges, steep on steep,

Thronging the sky—how shuddering as they leap

The impetuous waters go their fated way,

And mourn in mountain chasms, and as they stray

By many a magic town and marble tower,

As those that still unreconciled obey,

Sigh in the silence of the midnight hour.

Listen—the quiet darkness doth array

The toiling earth, and there is time to weep—

A deeper sound is mingled with the sweep

Of streams and winds that whisper far away.

Oh listen! where the populous cities lay

Low in the lap of sleep their ancient dower,

The changeless spirit of our changeful clay

Sighs in the silence of the midnight hour.

Sigh, watcher for a dawn remote and gray,

Mourn, journeyer to an undesirèd deep,

Eternal sower, thou that shalt not reap,

Immortal, whom the plagues of God devour.

Mourn—'tis the hour when thou wert wont to pray.

Sigh in the silence of the midnight hour.

PASSING

With thoughts too lovely to be true,
With thousand, thousand dreams I strew
The path that you must come.   And you
    Will find but dew.

I set an image in the grass,
A shape to smile on you.   Alas!
It is a shadow in a glass,
    And so will pass.

I break my heart here, love, to dower
With all its inmost sweet your bower.
What scent will greet you in an hour?
    The gorse in flower.

THE SONGS OF MYRTIS

I

LEND me the lyre again,

    The long forsaken !

One tone it must retain,

One song of all the store

I gave to it of yore

    Sleeps there to waken.

Wreathe me the lyre again !

    Moonflowers and sorrel

Gather by stream and plain,

Weaving a thousand flowers

Under the wild-rose bowers,

    But not the laurel.

Give me the lyre again !

As Heaven that sent it

Sucks from the earth her rain,

So from the trembling lyre

My soul shall drink the fire

That once she lent it.

II

LEND me thy wings, O dove,

But for a day,

And I will fly away,

Fly to my love.

Fearst thou I shall delay ?

Ah no, thou needst not fear,

Because though I should stay

But for a moment's space,

To look upon his face,

I shall return with love enough to last a year.

III

WHEN the world's asleep,

I awake and weep,

    Deeply sighing say,

    "Come, O break of day,

Lead my feet in my beloved's way."

When the morning breaks,

When the world awakes,

    Then a dream too dear

    Haunts me like a fear,

And as one in sleep I linger here.

If some star of heaven

Led him by at even,

    If some magic fate

    Brought him, should I wait,

Or fly within and bid them close the gate ?

IV

THE weary moon goes down into the West

      , As one that fain would rest,

And nothing now is waking in the skies

         Except the luminous eyes

Of stars that watch thee where thou wanderest.

         Wilt thou not also rest?

Now all the earth lies hushed in shadowy sleep,

         City and plain and steep;

Only the river journeying from afar

         Towards the Northern star

Rolls through the slumbering world its waters deep,

         That whisper to thee "Sleep."

And now is peace in that belovèd breast,

Peace, thè long absent guest;

For fear is dead, and sorrow sleeps forgot,

Love only slumbers not,

Love wakes for thee that doubting tarriest.

Wilt thou not also rest?

TASSO TO LEONORA

I

REPROACH me not because the many chide,

Calling me prouder than an Emperor's son,

For so the shepherds called Endymion,

When he had won the mateless moon to bride.

Proud?—Oh, a monarch must forget his pride,

On whom the light of such a love hath shone,

Showing him worth but dim oblivion,

A mortal set at an Immortal's side.

Rather one face, one hour, one master-thought

Stamped on the body and soul of him he bore,

And the world's business like a distant roar

To that tense mind his slackened senses brought.

And men he scorned not, save as the unborn

Or the forgetful dead sleeping appear to scorn.

II

No, there is none in all the earth save thee,

And never was, not through the length of time.

One is the sea whose everlasting chime

Cradles the world, however variously

Named on its sundered shores, and thou, my sea,

Streamest through every spiritual clime ;   ⟨

The kings of thought, the laurelled lords of rhyme,

Are names of thine or silent shades to me.

Thou to this heart canst never more be mute,

Though of that dumb fraternity of Death,

While there is sweetness in the viol and lute

And power in speech of man, and while with breath

Drawn from the world's worn air I fan the flame

That shatters and consumes and re-creates this frame.

III

I SHALL forget thee—yes, I shall forget

Thee and the Heavens that glorify the night,

Those silver summits trembling in the light

Of the descended moon, suns that have set,

Earth and the shoreless waters, all that yet

Has winged my soul for her tempestuous flight—

And dreams they send to seek me shall but light

On some gray stone wreathed with the violet.

Mingling thy dust with men that knew thee not,

Of me forgetful then thou'lt not complain,

And all we were shall be so much forgot

They who the history of our days rehearse

Shall call my grief a phantom of the brain,

Thy name a flower wrought on a poet's verse.

IV

THOU art a sword that's sheathèd in my heart,

To be by no adventure drawn again,

A divine vintage flooding every vein

With an immortal joy, even such thou art.

The Mænad Hours amid their dancing start

With haggard eyes from that empurpling stain.—

"See! Is it wine or blood?" they shriek in vain,

And heavily with garments dyed depart.

The Muse's self, the fierce relentless Muse

Art thou, that doth in love of man delight,

Kindling upon the lips her kisses choose

A flame that shall eternally be bright,

Fanned by Mnemosynè with fervent breath,

And watched by those grim guardians, Time and Death.

NOCTURNE

THE desolate heath

Over the sea

Is the place for me

When night is near,

When a wind upleaps

Seaward and sweeps

The horizon clear.

Widening beneath

Darkens the heath.

Sullen and far

Hark how they roar,

Waves of the shore,

Trees of the wood.

Heaven in her cloud,

Earth in her shroud,

Sullenly brood.

Smiles a white star

Silent and far.

Under the height

Yonder a glare

Reddens the air,

Where in the bay

Rigging and spars

Glow with their stars,

City and quay

Glitter to-night

Under the height.

O but for me

Purple of pine

In a sandy chine,

When the night-wind's breath

Will bare us soon

The wan young moon.

A desolate heath

Over the sea

Is the place for me.

THE EARTH ANGEL

BELOVED spirit, whom the angels miss,
While those heaven-wand'ring wings thou foldest here,
Love musing on thee, Love whose shadow is fear,
Divines thee born of fairer worlds than this,
And fain ere long to re-assume their bliss.
Stay, wingèd soul! for earth, this human sphere,
Claims thee her own, her light that storms swept clear,
Her righteousness that love, not peace, shall kiss.
'Twas out of time thou camest to be ours,
And dead men made thee in the darkling years,
Thy tenderness they bought for thee with tears,
Pity with pain that nothing could requite,
And all thy sweetness springs like later flowers
Thick on the field of some forgotten fight.

GENIUS LOCI

PEACE, Shepherd, peace! What boots it singing on?

Since long ago grace-giving Phœbus died,

And all the train that loved the stream-bright side

Of the poetic mount with him are gone

Beyond the shores of Styx and Acheron,

In unexplorèd realms of night to hide.

The clouds that strew their shadows far and wide

Are all of Heaven that visits Helicon.

Yet here, where never muse or god did haunt,

Still may some nameless power of Nature stray,

Pleased with the reedy stream's continual chant

And purple pomp of these broad fields in May.

The shepherds meet him where he herds the kine,

And careless pass him by whose is the gift divine.

GHOSTS

WHERE the columned cliffs far out have planted
  Their daring shafts in the Northern foam,
There hangs a castle that should be haunted,
  A ruin meet for a spectre's home.

For heavily in the caverns under
  The hidden tide like a muffled drum
Beats distinct through the level thunder
  Of the wintry waste whence storm-winds come.

And fire has blackened the mouldering rafter,
  And stairs have crumbled from bolted doors ;
At night there's a sound of wail and laughter,
  And footsteps crossing the creaking floors.

And in and out through the courts forsaken

    Wild shapes are drifted from hall to hall,

With a trumpet sound the towers are shaken,

    And banners flutter along the wall.

'Tis but the storms and the seas enchant it,

    Its ghosts are shadow and wind and spray.

If ever a phantom used to haunt it,

    That too was mortal and passed away.

The ghosts have found where the hills embosom

    A windless garden—they walk at noon,

When the beds and branches burn with blossom,

    And hardly wait for the rising moon.

When the starry charm of the night is broken,

    And the day but lives as a child unborn,

They pass with echoes of words once spoken

    And silent footsteps and eyes forlorn.

E

They seem as shadows of morn and even,

For ever fading to come again ;

They are as shadows of tempest driven,

Stormily sighing across the plain.

For these depart as the rest departed,

The garden under the hill shall be

As ghost-forsaken, as past-deserted

As the castle over the Northern sea.

TO THE EARTH

MISTRESS and slave of the sun,

Dancer with shining feet,

Gladly thou springest to greet

The year that is new begun.

Huntress who fliest with fleet

Hounds of the glittering air,

Again thou risest to chase the phantom year to its lair.

Long ere the threescore and ten

Pass us, the sum of our years,

Empty their pageant appears,

Old to the children of men.

April with laughter and tears

Tells a monotonous tale,

Winds of the Autumn in vain wildly and solemnly

wail.

Thou whom the ages bereave

Autumn on Autumn, behold,

Thou art not weary or cold;

Eagerly dost thou receive

Sunshine and rain as of old,

Comest again as a bride

Crowned with immortal delight, dead to the years that

have died.

Hear, O ye planets, her voice !

The vast and jubilant strain

Mountain and ocean and plain

Utter when she doth rejoice.

Surely the sound shall attain

Through sunless spaces afar,

Till it touch the silver heart of some high enthronèd star.

No—for thyself is the tale,

But for thine own hast thou sung.

Often the meadows among,

Laid by the stream in the frail

Shadow of April, there rung

Round me the voice of delight,

Murmur immense of the Earth joying alone in her
      might.

Once like a lover I heard,

Once like a lover I pressed

Kiss after kiss on thy breast,

Once all the rapture that stirred,

Streamed from the South and the West,

Flamed from the field and the sky,

Seemed for my heart to exult, seemed to my soul to reply.

Ah, could one bosom, one brain

Half of thine ecstasy hold ?

Lifetime of mortal unfold

One of thy mysteries ?   Vain,

Vain was the dream.   As of old

Messengers worn with the way

Fell at the Delphian's gate, fall I before thee to-day.

Hark how the Pythoness cries !

Priest to interpret is none,

Never a word to be won

Out of the rushing replies

Echoes pursue ere they're done.

Only I know 'twas a song

Passed me, escaped ere it taught me too the joy of the
strong.

Well mayst thou, Mother, be glad,

Great in a quenchless belief,

Well may we grow in our brief

Journey indifferent or sad.

Witnessing often the leaf

Broaden and wither, we see

Never the full up-shoot and branching growth of the tree.

Thou hearest the giant heart

Of a forest beating low

In the seed that faint winds sow

On an island far apart ;

And thou canst measure the slow

Lapse of the glittering sea,

Where it falls and clings round the land like a robe at a

bather's knee.

Yea, thou hast witnessed the whole

Agelong up-building of things ;

Through the ephemeral Springs

One indestructible soul,

Sleepless, unwearied, that brings

Order from chaos at length,

Out of the fading and weak infinite splendour and

strength.

THE DEATH OF HJÖRWARD

THE Norns decreed in their high home,

"Hjörward the king must die to-day,"—

A mighty man, but old and gray

With housing long on the gray foam,

And driving on their perilous way

His hungry dragon-herd to seek

Their fiery pasture, and to wreak

On southern shrines with flame and sword

The wrath of Asgard's dreadful lord.

Seven days king Hjörward then had kept

His place in silence on his throne,

Seven nights had left him there alone,

Watching while all the palace slept,

Wan in the dawn and still as stone.

But when they said, "The King must die,"

A shout such as in days gone by

Shook the good ship when swords were swung,

Broke from his heart and forth he sprung.

"Sword, sword and shield!" he cried, "and thou

Haste, let the wingèd ship fly free.

Yonder there shivers the pale sea,

Impatient for the plunging prow,

I hear the shrill wind call to me—

Hark, how it hastens from the East,

'Why tarriest thou?' it cries, 'the feast

To-night in Odin's hall is spread,

They wait thee there, the armèd dead."

"They wait me there l   Ho, sword and shield !

What hero-faces throng the gate !

Not long nor vainly shall ye wait.

I too have not been weak to wield

The heavy brand, I too am great,

Hjörward am I. 'No funeral car

Slow rolling, but a ship of war

Swift on the wind and racing wave,

Bears me to feast among the brave.

"Slaves, women, shall not sail with me,

Nor broidered stuffs, nor hoarded gold,

But men, my liegemen from of old,

Strong men to ride the unbroken sea,

And arms such as befit the bold.

Come forth, my steed, thou fierce and fleet,

Once more thy flying hoofs shall beat

The level way along the strand,

The hard bright sea-forsaken sand."

So the horse Halfi came, and rose

The hounds that wont to hunt with him,

Shaggy of hide and lithe of limb.

And we too followed where repose

The dragon-ships in order grim,

Hastening together to let slip

Svior, the dark shield-girdled ship,

That like a live thing from the steep

Fled eagerly into the deep.

Fly fast to-day, proud ship, fly fast,

Scatter the surge and drink the spray;

Hjörward is at thy helm to-day

For the last time, and for the last

Last time thou treadst the windy way.

The oarsmen to the chiming oar

Chant their hoarse song, and on the shore

The folk are silent watching thee

Speeding across the wide cold sea.

The wind that rose with day's decline

Rent the dim curtain of the west ;

Clear o'er the water's furthest crest

We saw a sudden splendour shine,

A flying flame that smote the breast

And high head of the mailèd King,

His hoary beard and glittering

Great brand in famous fights renowned,

And those grim chiefs that girt him round.

"The gate," he muttered, "lo ! the gate,"

Staring upon the sky's far gold.

Yea, the wild clouds about it rolled

Showed like the throned and awful state

Of gods whose feet the waves enfold,

Whose brows the voyaging tempests smite,

Who wait, assembled at the bright

Valhalla doors, the sail that brings

This last and mightiest of kings.

As swift before the wind we drave,

We surely heard from far within

Their shining battlements the din

Of that proud sword-play of the brave ;

And Hjörward cried, " The games begin,

The clang of shield on shield I hear.

Wait, sons of Odin, wait your peer !"

Then as that sudden splendour fled,

With one great shout the King fell dead.

And as some falcon struck in flight

Reels from her course, and dizzily

Beats with loose pinions down the sky,

So Svior reeled 'twixt height and height

Of mounting waves, and heavily

Plunged in the black trough of the sea ;

And o'er her helmless, full of glee,

The roaring waters leapt and fell,

Sweeping swift souls of men to Hell.

We seized the helm and lowered the mast,

And shorewards steered thro' night and wind ;

We seemed like loiterers left behind

By some bright pageant that had passed

Within and left to us the blind

Shut gates and twilight ways forlorn.

And coldly rose the strange new morn,

Ere to the watchers on the shore

We cried, " The King returns no more."

Return, ah ! once again return !

Cross the frail bridge at close of day,

And pale along the crimson way

Of sunset when the first stars burn,

Ride forth, thou king-born—look and say

If on the wide earth stretched beneath

Thou seest any house of death,

High sepulchre where monarchs be,

Like thine up-built beside the sea.

Far have I journeyed from the moan

Of northern waters, wandering

By tombs of many a famous king,

Where swathed in shrouds and sealed in stone

They slumber, and the tapers fling

A dimness o'er them, and the drone

Of praying priests they hear alone ;

Shut out from earth and bounteous sky,

And all the royal life gone by.

But Hjörward, clothed in shining mail,

Holds kingly state even where he died,

At Svior's helm.   On either side

The hoary chiefs who loved to sail

In youth with him sit full of pride,

Leaned on their arms and painted shields

Dim from a thousand battle-fields,

Looking upon the King, and he

Turns his helmed brows towards the sea.

Across his knees his naked brand

Is laid, and underneath his feet

The Goth horse Halfi, and the fleet

F

Great hounds he loved beneath his hand,

And when the storms arise there beat

Salt surges up against his grave.

He surely sometimes feels the brave

Ship Svior quiver in her sleep,

Dreaming she treads the windy deep.

There overhead year after year

The moorland turf and thyme shall grow,

Above the horizon faint and low

The same wild mountain summits peer ;

The same gray gleamy sea shall sow

With foam the level leagues of sand,

And peace be with that warrior band,

Till dim below the bright abodes

Gather the twilight of the gods.

RAMESES

From the ancient Poem of Pentaur, the Egyptian scribe.

KING RAMESES marched to the Northward, to the
borders of Kadesh he came,

He marched like his father Mentu for Orontes that
waters the same

With the troop that has "Victory Bringer" and the
name of the King for its name.

But ere he was come to the city the Vile One or Khita
arose,

From the shores of the sea unto Khita he summoned
King Rameses' foes,

They gathered as grasshoppers gather, like locusts
  assembled they lay

And covered the mountains and valleys, and no man
  was left by the way.

There led them the lord of the Khita and bore with
  him treasures untold,

He emptied the realm of its treasure, he stript it of
  silver and gold.

Like sand were the men and the horses, he had gathered
  them all to the war ;

The well-armed champions of Khita stood three upon
  every car.

Countless they crouched in their ambush, they were
  hidden west of the town,

They rushed on the troop of the sun-god, and horse and
  foot went down.

Yea, unawares they had smitten the host of the King
   and possessed

Kadesh that lies by Orontes, on the bank of the stream
   to the West.

King Rameses heard and he armed him, like Mentu he
   rose in his pow'r,

He seized his arms for the battle, he clutched them like
   Bar in his hour,

And swift from their stalls in the vanguard, from the
   stable of Rameses came

His steeds that were mighty to bear him—"Victory in
   Thebes" was their name.

Fast, fast in his fury he drave them, he brake through
   the ranks of the foe,

The King he alone and none other, then he turned to
   behold them, and lo!

The chariots of Khita by thousands had compassed him
  round and there lay

The hosts of the Vile One of Khita as a bar in King
  Rameses' way,

The tribes of the sea and the mountain, the numberless
  nations from far,

And the bravest champions of Khita stood three upon
  every car.

"Was there one of my chariots with me? Of my
  captains and lords was there one?

Nay, but they fled from the battle, and Pharaoh
  remained there alone."

Then Rameses cried unto Ammon: "Deniest thou,
  father, thy son?

Wherein have I sinned against Ammon, what deed
  without him have I done?

Are the monuments vain I have made thee? For
nought was the sacrifice slain?

The thousands of bulls for thine altars and captives in
throngs for thy fane,

And lands hast thou counted as nothing? and treasures
as utterly vain?

All odorous woods I have brought thee, the incense was
sweet in my hand.

I finished thy courts, and thy gateways of stone over-
shadow the land,

With masts I adorned thee the portals, 'tis I who have
brought unto thee

The obelisks hewn at Syene, and galleys that bear o'er
the sea

The wealth of the world to thine altars the hand of King
Rameses steers—

I have given thee stone everlasting, a house for a million
of years.

Such gifts were they given aforetime? Of old hast thou
witnessed the same?

On him who rejecteth thy counsels, on him be confusion
and shame,

But I who have honoured thee, Ammon, my father I
call on thy name.

The multitudes gather against me, I stand amid nations
unknown,

I stand here alone with no other, they are many and I
am alone;

My chariots and horsemen have left me, they heeded me
not when I cried,

But better than millions of horsemen, ay better than
sons at my side,

And more than a thousand of brothers though marshalled
about me they fought,

Is Ammon who maketh the labour of multitudes even as
nought.

Behold it is thou that hast done it, I blame not thy

    counsels, I cry

To the ends of the earth, I invoke thee ! "

                        The house of Hermonthis on high

Re-echoed the voice of my crying, he heard and he

    came like the wind,

I shouted for joy at his coming, as hastening he called

    from behind ;

"It is I, it is Ammon thy father, I am eager to help

    thee my son,

The lord and the lover of heroes, I am Ra the victorious

    one.

My heart has rejoiced in thy valour, I stretch forth my

    hand to the fray,

And better than millions of horsemen shall Ammon

    befriend thee to-day."

He spake and the word was accomplished. Like Mentu
    I shoot to the right,

I grasp to the left in my fury, I break them as Bar in
    his might.

Two thousand five hundred the chariots, I see them,
    they shall not withstand,

I am there in the midst with my horses, I trample them
    as it were sand.

They found not their hands for the battle, amazement
    befell them and fear,

They slackened the bowstring before me, they knew
    not to handle the spear ;

Yea, one on another I hurled them and headlong they
    fell in the flood,

As crocodiles fall in the river so fell they, I drank of
    their blood.

King Rameses said, " 'Tis my pleasure that none shall
    return from the fight,

Not one shall arise of the fallen, nor any look back unto
   flight."

And there was the Vile One of Khita, he stood 'mid his
   legions to see ;

Beholding the valour of Pharaoh he trembled, he turned
   him to flee.

The King was alone.   Then he mustered his bravest
   and sent them to slay

King Rameses, numberless horsemen assembled in
   battle array.

I say to my hand, "Thou shalt taste them," and, lo, in
   a moment of space

I spring like a flame to devour them—they perish each
   one in his place.

I hear through the wind of my rushing how one of them
   cries to the other,

"Not a man, not a man is against us, beware of the god,
O my brother !

The mighty have seen him and straightway their arrows
have dropped from the bow,

They lift not a hand when he cometh, his countenance
layeth them low.

Like Ra in the front of the morning his quiver is laden
with flame,

'Tis Sechet consumes us before him, 'tis Bar that
possesses his frame."

Like a griffin the King has pursued them, they come to
the meeting of ways.

They flee but they cannot escape him, he calls to his
men as he slays,

" Ho, courage my horsemen and footmen ! Look back
for a little and see

How I conquer alone with no other but Ammon that
fighteth for me."

My charioteer, even Menna, was with me and he was
afraid,

In the press of the chariots he trembled, his spirit was
greatly dismayed.

"O Prince and protector of Egypt, O gracious and
mighty," he saith,

"Thou fightest alone against many, how now canst thou
save us our breath?

King Rameses, gracious and mighty, we cannot escape
from our death."

But Rameses cried to him, "Courage, ho, courage, my
charioteer!

Behold, as a hawk I will pierce them and rend them,
why then shouldst thou fear?

And what to thy heart are these herdsmen, since Ra will
not brighten his face,

On millions of such, the ungodly, he loveth to humble
their race."

King Rameses rushed on the vanguard, he brake
through the ranks of the foe,

Six times he has sundered and broken the ranks of the
Khita and low

He has laid them, the caitiffs of Khita, they trembled
before him and quailed,

They fled but they could not escape him, like Bar in his
hour he prevailed.

And now when my horsemen and footmen beheld me
they worshipped afar,

They praised me as Mentu the mighty, the sword un-
resisted of Ra ;

For the god, yea, the god, was beside me, 'twas he who
had brought it to pass

That nations were scattered before me and were to my
horses as grass.

They marched from the camp in the evening, they came
in their wonder and stood

Where I brake through the tribes and the mighty of
Khita lay whelmed in their blood,

The sons of the chief and the kinsfolk—and morning
arose on the plain,

It lighted the field, and in Kadesh was nowhere to tread
for the slain.

A MAY SONG

O SHEPHERDESS come,
    Come wander away !
For young is the morning
    And fresh is the May.

A green world about us,
    A blue world on high,
White bloom on the branches,
    White clouds in the sky.

O were we two poets
    We'd loiter to sing
Through the sun-wakened city
    The joy of the Spring.

And were we two painters

　We surely should stay

To capture for ever

　The fresh-coloured May.

But beauty of May-time

　Escapes from our praise ;

We should miss our sweet meaning

　And miss the sweet days.

There's piping and singing

　In thicket and grass,

And murmur in meadows

　Of streams as they pass,

And high in the Heaven

　There's a lark that upstarts

With the song of the May

　And the song of our hearts.

G

O Shepherdess come,

Come wander away!

For young is the morning

And fresh is the May.

TWILIGHT

Come, let us go,

For now the gray and silent eve is low,

The river reaches gleam,

And dimly blue in windings of the stream

Its heavy rushes bow.

The day is past, the world is dreaming now,

The world is dreaming now, let us too dream.

And dreaming be

The vision of our souls like this we see,

Where unsubstantial skies

Blend with the Earth's obscure realities.

Let us recall the blind

Forewandered years and round their temples bind

Fresh coronals of lovelier memories.

For dreaming here
We shall remember joys that never were,
That might and might not be ;
One rich remembrance with its alchemy
Transmuting all Time's store,
Till the sad years exult and deem they bore
Only the long, long love 'twixt thee and me.

AT THE BARRICADE

Was it a living woman there,

    Crouched by the barricade?

I said, "We have shelter and food to spare,

Come in and rest, for the game is played."

For a moment she lifted her heavy head,

Lifted her heavily drooping hair,

For a moment as a bayonet blade

Gleams in a flying moonbeam, gleamed

Her face upon me passionate-eyed—

But calm as a girl's at her needle seemed

Her voice as she replied.

" 'Tis not worth while to rest," she said,

" I shall so soon be dead."

Sunny and still was the long white street;

You might have fancied the gracious and gay

City was sleeping away the heat

　　Of a cloudless summer day.

Not a soul save her in the street—

But hark ! There's the regular tramp of marching feet !

They are coming, the Versaillais.

By bridge and boulevard marching on,

Like conquerors proud of a battle won,

Like avengers glad of a vengeance done ;

And never a man to meet them there !

Will no one face them ? Will no one dare

Fire a last shot for the barricade ?

Yes—a shot, another and yet another,

One racing close on the heels of the other,

Six flying straight for the ranks, that swayed

Back for a startled moment, then

Hoarsely roaring for slaughter and strife,

With a tiger bound took the barricade.

Throbbed in their ears as on they came

The low fierce voice of a distant flame ;

Pouring over with bullet and knife,

They were ready to clash with a murderous horde,

Ready to close with desperate men,

Eager to struggle and smite and wade

Onward as conquerors, deep in blood.

But not to face one woman, one

Waiting them there alone..

As a tiger the lone hunter's eye

Baulks in its spring and holds amazed,

Growling, crouched reluctantly,

Thus paused they and thus gazed.

Still as herself the captain stood

Awhile and then there clashed his sword,

Suddenly dropping into its sheath.

"You're a brave woman, you!

Two of my men shot dead!"   "But two?

God forgive me!   It is too few.

I should have taken a life for a life.

All of us, all you have done to death,

The father first, but the boys fought well.

'They will live to avenge us yet,' I said.

Two of the four at Neuilly fell

And two—just here I found them dead.

But I not yet am wholly slain—

Finish your work.   Fire once again."

YOUNG WINDEBANK

THEY shot young Windebank just here,
    By Merton, where the sun
Strikes on the wall. 'Twas in a year
    Of blood the deed was done.

At morning from the meadows dim
    He watched them dig his grave.
Was this in truth the end for him,
    The well-beloved and brave?

He marched with soldier scarf and sword,
    Set free to die that day,
And free to speak once more the word
    That marshalled men obey.

But silent on the silent band

    That faced him stern as death,

He looked and on the summer land

    And on the grave beneath.

Then with a sudden smile and proud

    He waved his plume and cried,

"The king! the king!" and laughed aloud,

    "The king! the king!" and died.

Let none affirm he vainly fell,

    And paid the barren cost

Of having loved and served too well

    A poor cause and a lost :

He in the soul's eternal cause

    Went forth as martyrs must—

The kings who make the spirit laws

    And rule us from the dust.

Whose wills unshaken by the breath

Of adverse Fate endure,

To give us honour strong as death

And loyal love as sure.

AN EASTERN LEGEND

In cloisters dim and haunted

    She met me and I said ;

" Art thou the queen enchanted

    Of whom long since I read?

Whose heart a great magician

    Has hidden from her birth,

Either in the deep ocean

    The forest or the earth."

She seemed a monarch's daughter

    Her body like a palm,

Her voice like silver water

    That speaks when all is calm.

She answered, " It is hidden."

And smiling dreamily,

" But messengers unbidden

Bring news of it to me.

The wildest nights creep hither

All dumb, with muffled feet,

Yet through the halcyon weather

I often feel a fleet

Fresh wind about me blowing

And power within my breast,

As of the great seas flowing

That do not ask for rest.

" O then my heart is driven

I know 'twixt shore and shore.

The moon is large in heaven,

The gathering waters roar.

"The sullen trees unshaken

　　Keep charmèd shadow here,

Nor know how woods awaken

　　Afar when spring is near.

Yet from the boughs wild voices

　　Are sometimes calling me ;

The soul of me rejoices,

　　The frozen blood runs free,

And needs I must go roaming

　　And sing and laugh alone,

While through the magic gloaming

　　Strange lights are tossed and blown.

"'Tis when mid forest branches

　　My heart keeps watch and sees

As wind the water blanches,

　　How spring makes red the trees.

About my trancèd slumber

    At moments rise and sweep

Dread visions without number

    That battle and that weep;

And more than men who waken

    I know of Death and Birth,

Because my heart is taken

    And buried in the Earth."

I said : " The habitation

    Of dreams is not for thee.

Tell me what incantation,

    What toil can set thee free ?

Surely thy soul desireth

    The sun and moon for light,

Ay, and the glow that fireth

    The festal halls at night.

The springtime in its sweetness,

    The summer in its strength,

The world in its completeness

    Thou shalt possess at length."

. Pale, with a solemn gesture

    Either of prayer or pain,

She wrapped her in her vesture,

    Nor looked on me again.

I heard a hollow crying

    In all the palace around,

Like echoes far replying

    To unperceivèd sound,

A clash along the arches

    Long drawn on either side,

As of a guard that marches—

    It rose and passed and died.

Her saw I not, nor even

    Shadows of living things,

Save that without the seven

    Great sphinxes stirred their wings ;

They who with sleepless vision

    For ever contemplate,

Smiling in still derision,

    The world and men and fate.

THE ETERNAL

EARTH is His garment and also heaven,

Its skirts are broadened from day to day

By a million shining shuttles driven

Through a formless woof till a form is given,

And the suns break forth like the buds in May.

The rushing river, the pulsing ocean,

The clouds when they clash and find a voice,

Are as folds that heave with a heart's emotion,

That cling and swing with the dancers' motion

When the sunburnt girls of the South rejoice.

Lo, when the vision of Man perceiveth

Beneath what all living eyes can see,

The mighty and jubilant heart that heaveth,

The Life that the dance of the forces weaveth,

He trembles perceiving and bows the knee.

And first he worships the Life in Nature,

He fashions him gods of earth and sky,

Strong, senseless lords of the sentient creature,

He lends them language and name and feature,

And an ear to hear when the nations cry.

He rears him altars where clouds are driven

Like dumb white surf on the crags below.

Set in the midst of the spacious heaven

They watch while the world is tempest-riven,

How the lamps of God serenely glow.

But the years go by that deaden wonder,

And mute in the desert of the mind

He sits at last, while the wind and thunder

Sweep past and the deep Earth trembles under,

Yet the Spirit therein he cannot find.

He cries, " Art silent and dark for ever,

Thou Fear, Thou Light of the Universe?

Wilt Thou as soul from body sever

The might of Thy dread from Man's endeavour?

Speak to us Thunderer, though Thou curse!"

Answer, O Spirit, in exultation!

Spirit of God that still doth move

Over the deep of our Creation,

Spirit of Man in aspiration,

Answer with Mercy and Law and Love!

THE END.

Printed by R. & R. CLARK, *Edinburgh.*

" The writer has a keen appreciation of nature and a deep knowledge of character, especially rustic character. You breathe fresh air and rustic life in every page. There is much power, pathos, and quiet humour, besides a considerable dramatic force."—*Pall Mall Gazette.*

" One of the strongest, saddest, and most artistically written and constructed stories I have come across for a long time. There is a brilliant future before its author."—*Truth.*

" We should advise every one who reads this tale to read it twice, and to let no long time elapse between the first and second readings. The reader sits spellbound, and has little leisure to notice the fine touches of thought and expression which are to be found in almost every page."—*Oxford Magazine.*

" Here is the work of a poet, a true sonnet without verse, mournful to actual pain, tragic indeed, yet how true, how quiet, how pure ! A vignette, no doubt, in a very low key, and a very narrow range, but in that key and within that range, of the kith and kin of the Village Tragedies of the masters ; of George Eliot, Tourgéneff, Georges Sand, Tolstoi, Ohnet. . . . Yes! this is indeed the work of a poet ; full of intense pity for all that is pitiful in the common ; full of calm, resolute, piercing observation of men, circumstance, and English life ; full of melody and colour, though of sombre colour ; a tale told in an English speech as pure, simple, and pellucid as ever our best have used, and such as but few are now found to use."—Professor Frederic Harrison in the *Nineteenth Century.*